#1 "BWAAAAAAAAAAH!"

Thitaume - Writer
Romain Pujol - Artist
Gorobei - Colorist

PAPERCUTZ™
New York

ACKNOWLEDGMENTS

Thanks to François Tallec for trusting in us and for his oversight throughout the production of this volume.
Thanks also to Cédric Royer for his candidness and his many wise suggestions.
A big thanks to Romain Pujol and Gorobei who, by dint of talent and patience, succeeded in transforming my few ideas into superb comicbook pages.
A special thanks to MAD Fabrik Editions, who let me take my first steps in this profession and especially so to Araceli Cancino for her continued encouragement and helping hand.
Lastly, thanks to Magali for putting up with me on those days when inspiration was wanting.
I dedicate this book to my parents.

--Thitaume

Thanks to Thitaume and Gorobei for working enthusiastically along with me to make this book.
Thanks to François Tallec, Cédric Royet and Amy Jenkins for their support through the course of this adventure, as well as to my parents for their trust in me.
As for Julie and the readers of my blog, thanks for your patience and commitment.
I'd also like to thank Ubisoft for suggesting to me to rappel down from the heights of their company.
And lastly, I'd like to speak to you, yes, you, who with your sweaty hands are holding this volume, I congratulate you, you have good taste.
I dedicate this book to my family.

--Romain Pujol

RABBIDS #1 "BWAAAAAAAAAAH!"
Thitaume – Writer
Romain Pujol – Artist
Gorobei – Colorist
Joe Johnson – Translator

978-1-62991-048-2 Paperback Edition
978-1-62991-049-9 Hardcover Edition

Papercutz books may be purchased for business or promotional use. For information on bulk purchases please contact Macmillan Corporate and Premium Sales Department at (800) 221-7945 x5442.

PRINTED IN THE USA
SEPTEMBER 2014 BY Lifetouch Printing
5126 Forest Hills Ct. , Loves Park, IL 61111

DISTRIBUTED BY MACMILLAN
FIRST PAPERCUTZ PRINTING

STOP!

You're not at the *beginning* of the book.
To get there, please follow the directions on page **48**.

Thitaume -Pujol-

Thitaume -Pujol-

Thitaume -Pujol-

9

ThiTAUME -PUJOL-

THITAUME -PUJOL-

THITAUME -PUJOL-

IN ORDER TO TREAT THIS RABBID AS HUMANELY AS POSSIBLE...

TURNING THIS GRAPHIC NOVEL UPSIDE-DOWN IS STRICTLY PROHIBITED.

THANK YOU FOR UNDERSTANDING.

ThiTAUME -PuJOL-

THITAUME -PUJOL-

THITAUME -PUJOL-

THITAUME -PUJOL-

THITAUME -PUJOL-

THITAUME -PUJOL-

BWAAAH!

THITAUME -PUJOL-

PAINT

Thitaume -Pujol-

THITAUME -PUJOL

THiTAUME -PUJOL-

BWAAAH!

Thitaume -Pujol-

The Rabbids return in an all-new full-length adventure in RABBIDS #2 Coming Soon!

GOOD JOB!
You're Almost There!

Now, go to page 4 and start reading!